# TROUBLE
## in the Barkers' Class

Written and illustrated by

# TOMIE DEPAOLA

PUFFIN BOOKS

For Sara, Jennifer, Katrina, Maria
—and Bob and Mario.
They were ALL trouble in their classes!

PUFFIN BOOKS
Published by the Penguin Group
Penguin Young Readers Group, 345 Hudson Street, New York, New York 10014, U.S.A.
Penguin Group (Canada), 90 Eglinton Avenue East, Suite 700, Toronto, Ontario, Canada M4P 2Y3 (a division of Pearson Penguin Canada Inc.)
Penguin Books Ltd, 80 Strand, London WC2R 0RL, England
Penguin Ireland, 25 St Stephen's Green, Dublin 2, Ireland (a division of Penguin Books Ltd)
Penguin Group (Australia), 250 Camberwell Road, Camberwell, Victoria 3124, Australia (a division of Pearson Australia Group Pty Ltd)
Penguin Books India Pvt Ltd, 11 Community Centre, Panchsheel Park, New Delhi - 110 017, India
Penguin Group (NZ), Cnr Airborne and Rosedale Roads, Albany, Auckland 1310, New Zealand (a division of Pearson New Zealand Ltd)
Penguin Books (South Africa) (Pty) Ltd, 24 Sturdee Avenue, Rosebank, Johannesburg 2196, South Africa

Registered Offices: Penguin Books Ltd, 80 Strand, London WC2R 0RL, England

First published in the United States of America by G. P. Putnam's Sons, a division of Penguin Young Readers Group, 2003
Published by Puffin Books, a division of Penguin Young Readers Group, 2006

7  9  10  8  6

Copyright © Tomie dePaola, 2003
All rights reserved
The Barker Twins is a trademark of Penguin Group (USA) Inc.
Designed by Gina DiMassi.
Text set in Worcester Round Medium.
The art was done in transparent acrylics on Fabriano 140 lb. handmade watercolor paper.

THE LIBRARY OF CONGRESS HAS CATALOGED THE G. P. PUTNAM'S SONS EDITION AS FOLLOWS:
dePaola, Tomie.
Trouble in the Barkers' class / written and illustrated by Tomie dePaola.—1st ed.
p.   cm.
Summary: When a new girl in the Barkers' class, Carole Anne, acts like a bully, the students try talking
to her and ignoring her until Morgie finally discovers what is wrong and finds a way to fix it.
ISBN: 0-399-24164-7 (hc)
[1. Bullies–Fiction. 2. Behavior–Fiction. 3. Schools–Fiction. 4. Twins–Fiction.]
I. Title.
PZ7.D439Tt 2003 [E]–dc21 2003001280

Puffin Books ISBN 978-0-14-240585-7

Manufactured in China

Girls and boys," Ms. Shepherd said, "I have a surprise for you. A new student is joining our class tomorrow. Her name is Carole Anne. Let's make her feel really welcome. It's always hard to come into a new class after everyone else is here."

The class was excited about Carole Anne coming.
"Can I draw a Welcome Card for her, Ms. Shepherd?"
Morgie asked.

"That's a good idea, Morgie," his twin sister, Moffie, said.
"You are the best artist in our class." Moffie was very proud
of Morgie.

"Do you think she likes building with blocks?" Sally asked Moffie. She and Moffie built the tallest towers in the class.

"I hope she likes to play ball," Bobby said. Any game with a ball was Bobby's favorite.

"I wonder if she knows her colors, numbers, and how to spell her name," Moffie said.

"I'm going to invite her to my birthday party," Katrina said. "I hope she likes dinosaurs," Morgie said. "I'm going to bring T-Rex to school tomorrow to show her."

The next morning started out fine.

"Good morning, everyone," Ms. Shepherd said. "I'd like you all to meet Carole Anne."

The children smiled at her, but Carole Anne didn't smile back. She just looked away.

"I think she's shy," Moffie whispered to Sally.
"Maybe she's scared," Sara whispered to Jennifer.
"She's shorter than I thought," Morgie whispered to Billy.

Ms. Shepherd gave Carole Anne her books and showed her where to sit next to Morgie.

Morgie had made the Welcome Card for her, but Carole
Anne just threw it on the floor.

In the middle of the morning, the bell rang for recess.
"All right, class," Ms. Shepherd said. "Line up and we'll
go outside."

Moffie was at the front of the girls' line when she felt
someone shove her.

It was Carole Anne pushing her way to the head of the line.

"Hey," Moffie said, "you pushed me."

"So what?" Carole Anne said, and she walked to the playground.

"Gee," Sally said. "She's not very nice."

Billy and José were calling for Morgie to play ball with them.

But first Morgie wanted to show Carole Anne his dinosaur.
"This is T-Rex," Morgie said.

"You bring your dolls to school?" Carole Anne snickered.
"What a BABY."
Morgie just looked at her. He didn't know what to say.

After lunch, it was time for Independent Reading.
Everyone got to pick his or her own book.

"It's such a nice day, class," Ms. Shepherd said. "Let's take
our books outside."

On the way out, Carole Anne cut in line again.

"Hey," Sally said. "Stop pushing."

"Yes," the girls said, "we don't push at OUR school."

"Well, I do," Carole Anne said. "Who's going to stop me?"
And she pulled out Maria's bows.

Morgie was sitting under a tree with his special dinosaur book. Carole Anne marched up, grabbed the book, and ran off. "Stop, thief! Give me back my book," Morgie cried.

"Get it yourself, stupid," Carole Anne said.
And she threw the book into the bushes.
Billy and Bobby helped Morgie find his book.
"I wish she wasn't in our class," Billy said.
"Me too," Morgie said.

The next day, Carole Anne picked on Morgie again. He had just finished a drawing of Dinosaur Land when Carole Anne reached over and scribbled all over it in red crayon.

"Hey," Morgie said. "Why did you do that?"
Carole Anne just stuck her tongue out at him.

At home, Papa asked the twins about school.

"There's a new girl in class who's awful. Morgie has to sit next to her, and she keeps picking on him," Moffie said.

"She threw my dinosaur book in the bushes. Then today, she scribbled all over my drawing," Morgie said.

"Oh, dear," Mama said, "maybe you should speak to Ms. Shepherd."

"We don't want to be tattletales," the twins said, "but school sure isn't fun anymore."

"Well," Mama and Papa said, "maybe you and your friends can think of something to help."

"I help," their little adopted brother, Marcos, said. "*Conejito*—bunny—chase her away!"

"*Gracias*—thanks—Marcos," Morgie said. "But Moffie and I will figure something out."

The next morning before school, the children got together to talk about Carole Anne. They decided that the best thing to do was to leave her all alone.

"Let's not ask her to play jump rope with us," Sally said.

"Let's not ask her to play ball," Billy said.

"Let's not look at books with her," Sara and Jennifer said.

"And I'm not inviting her to my birthday party," Katrina said.

When Carole Anne tried to get to the front of the line, Moffie, Sally, and Sara stood in her way.

When Carole Anne called Morgie a name, Billy, Bobby, and José all whistled or hummed.

"We can't hear you," the boys said, and walked away.

Finally Carole Anne was all by herself. Everyone else was playing.

Ms. Shepherd saw what was happening.

"Class," she said, "why aren't you playing with Carole Anne? You're not being very friendly to our new classmate."

"But," the children said, "she's nasty to us!"

"She shoves," Sally said.

"She cuts in line," José said.

"She calls us names," Jennifer said.

"And she scribbles all over Morgie's beautiful drawings!" Moffie said.

"Really?" Ms. Shepherd said. "Carole Anne, is that true?"

"NO," Carole Anne said.

"Yes, it is," the children said.

Ms. Shepherd went over and sat down next to Carole Anne.

"Carole Anne, do you want to talk about this?" Ms. Shepherd asked.

"NO," Carole Anne said.

"I'll tell you what, everyone, let's all think about this over the weekend," Ms. Shepherd said. "We'll talk on Monday."

The next morning Morgie was out looking for rocks that looked like dinosaur eggs for Show-and-Tell. He thought he heard someone crying. He peeked behind the bushes. There was Carole Anne.

"What's the matter?" Morgie asked. "I didn't know you lived around here."

"I do," Carole Anne said, "but I went out for a walk and got lost."

"Well," Morgie said, "I'm looking for rocks that look like dinosaur eggs for Show-and-Tell on Monday. Do you want to help me? Then you can tell me where you live and I'll help you find your way home."

"Okay," Carole Anne said.

After they had found enough rocks and were walking along, Morgie asked Carole Anne, "Why are you so nasty at school? Don't you like our class?"

Carole Anne started talking, and they talked all the way to Carole Anne's house.

On Monday, it was Morgie's turn for Show-and-Tell.

"Carole Anne and I found all these rocks that look like dinosaur eggs. We painted them, and we have one for each of you. And one for you, too, Ms. Shepherd."

The children were surprised. How come Morgie and Carole Anne were friends?

"Carole Anne wants to tell you something," Morgie said.

"I'm sorry I was so nasty," Carole Anne said. "This is my second new school this year. I was the last one here, and I was afraid no one would like me. I thought I had to push and shove and cut into line so I wouldn't be last. I called you names before you could call me names. I was mad at Morgie because everyone likes him, and they don't like me."

Carole Anne took a big breath.

"I'm very sorry," she said. "I just want to be friends."

"She's my friend," Morgie said.

"She's mine too," Moffie said.

"Mine too!" Billy and Sally said.

"Ours too!" the class shouted.

"I'm very proud of all of you," Ms. Shepherd said.

"Great," Moffie and Morgie said.
"School is fun again!"